D*i*

Pr

DATE DUE

AUG 2 6 2008		
JUN 14 2010		
AUG 3 1 2011		

DEMCO 38-296

DISNEY
PRESS

N E W   Y O R K

To my friend and neighbor
Georgia Ruth Davis Handforth, with affection

Contents

Princess of Power

Chapter One

My Dojo

Breathe in. Step to the right. Pivot. Front punch. Slow spin kick to the left. Breathe out. Feet together, palms together. Bow. Breathe in and out. Done.

As I slowly raised my head after finishing my kata, I could feel a tingle of magic flowing in and around me. The air itself crackled as I stood in a line with the other kids in my tae kwan do group. The eight of us were facing a mirror-lined wall, as if we were in a ballet class. In the mirror, I met the eyes of one of my best friends, Jasmine Prentiss. One corner of her mouth tilted up ever so slightly, but it was enough for me to tell that she was feeling the same rush that I was. I stared straight ahead, paying attention to my breathing.

"Good," said our teacher, Sensei Kerry. She bowed sharply to us, and we quickly bowed back. "Three-minute break."

Our line melted as we started shaking out our muscles. I moved closer to Jasmine, and she grinned at me.

"Good form, Ms. Paula," she said.

"You too, Ms. Jasmine," I returned. I flapped the neckline of my gi to let some air in. Even though it was late September, it was still roasting-hot outside, and the dojo wasn't air-conditioned.

Since I have three minutes, I'll try to get you caught up ASAP. My name is Paula Pinto. I'm nine years old, in fourth grade at Orlando Elementary, and I live in a suburb of Orlando, Florida, called Willow Hill. I have five best friends: Jasmine, Yukiko Hayashi, Ariel Ramos, Isabelle Beaumont, and Ella O'Connnor. Ariel is also my *best* best friend.

Right now, Jasmine and I were at a Saturday class at our dojo. Tae kwan do (tie-kwan-doh) is a type of karate. A *gi* (with a hard *g*, as in *girl*) is the uniform we wear to practice in. A *dojo* is a place where you study martial arts—kind of like a dance studio. In fact, ballet and karate have some things in common. Jasmine takes both ballet and tae kwan do, so she should know.

Usually Jasmine and I take tae kwan do only once a week, on Tuesday afternoons after school. But right now we were getting ready to advance to another level with our skills. We both had orange belts, and in a few weeks we would try to qualify for our green belts. (At first, a tae kwan do student doesn't have any belt at all. Then you get a white belt, then yellow, then orange. After that comes green, blue, purple, brown, and black. I couldn't wait to become a black belt, but I knew it would take several more years.)

Since we had a belt test coming up, we both wanted to cram in as much extra practice time as possible.

Besides being way cool and challenging, tae kwan do is good exercise, for both my mind and my body. After every class I come home all sweaty from a good workout, and sometimes even sore. And my mind feels clear and focused afterward because of the intense attention I have to pay in class.

At the edge of the studio, I grabbed my water bottle

and took a couple of deep swigs. My long dark hair was pulled back into a tight bun, but some wispies had escaped and were plastered to my forehead. Looking at the mirrored wall, I brushed them off my forehead. Then I saw him.

"*Whoosh!*" The breath left his lungs in a hard, fast stream as he punched with his right fist. I sighed. While the rest of us were drinking water, drying off, and catching our breath, Jam was still working out hard, all by himself.

Jam is the one thing that I don't like about tae kwan do. When I was a white belt and a yellow belt, I never saw him. Now that I'm an orange belt, my classes and Jam's are overlapping more.

"Yah!" Jam bit out as he aimed a high kick at his image in the mirror.

Jam is a blue belt. I don't know how old he is (older than me), or where he goes for regular school. All I know is that he bugs me. For one thing, it seems as if every time I see him, he's making dumb remarks about "baby belts." I mean, *so* unfair! Like he was never a white belt! For another thing, he seems to have a grudge against *me* in particular. Go figure! I haven't done anything to him! But when we're in class together, I can feel his cold blue eyes watching me, waiting for me to mess up. (Everyone messes up sometimes.) It ticks me off. And finally (I hate to admit this because it isn't great for my karma), I can't stand the fact that he's really, really good at tae kwan do. I would feel better if he were lame in class. Then I could feel sorry for him and try to help him. But I could tell that Jam needed my help about as much as my pet raccoon, Meeko, needs lessons in badness.

"Attention!" said Sensei Kerry, and we all snapped to, standing in our proper positions. Class began again.

After class, Jasmine and I changed into normal clothes. I don't know if you've ever been to Orlando, Florida, but if you have, you know that it's really hot here most of the time. I actually like it, though some people complain about it.

Anyway, we put our gis and safety gear into our duffels and strapped them to the back of our bikes. Jasmine was riding home with me because later on today I was hosting a Disney Girls sleepover at my house. (I'll explain about the DGs in a minute.)

"Where is he?" Jasmine asked, peering through her sunglasses down the street.

"He'll be here," I said. We were waiting for my brother, Damon, who had said he would ride home with us. Damon's fourteen, and in ninth grade at Orlando High. He's an awesome big brother.

After ten minutes, though, I guessed Damon had gotten stuck in a pickup basketball game or something, so we got on our bikes and started to pedal home. Through the big window of the dojo, I could see Jam still practicing by himself in front of the mirror.

"At least he's working out with his favorite person," said Jasmine, and I grinned.

Just then Damon pedaled up to us. He was panting and red-faced, and his dark ponytail was limp with sweat. "Sorry, guys," he said as he turned and rode alongside me. "Something came up and I forgot the time."

"No prob," I said. We pedaled home. I was already looking forward to tonight's sleepover.

Chapter Two

My Tribe

Ariel was waiting for us when we got to my house. It's so cool that my *best* best friend lives right around the block from me. One corner of her yard almost touches one corner of my yard. Although my house is pretty small, we have a big lot, and our yard goes way back.

"Hey, guys," she said as we pedaled up. "How was class?" She was eating a Popsicle, which was dripping, and I noticed a line of small black ants already heading for the sweet juice. That's Florida for you—teeming with wildlife.

"Great," said Jasmine, slowing to a stop and getting off her bike.

"Fine," I said. I was still troubled about Jam, and I was irritated with myself about it. I had to quit thinking about him. It was Disney Girls time!

"I hope it's okay that I'm like three hours early for the sleepover. I was bored at home," said Ariel. *Slurp, slurp.*

"No, I was going to call you anyway," I said, hopping off my own bike. Ariel followed me, Damon, and Jasmine as we wheeled our bikes around back and locked them in the garage.

"Later," said Damon as he trotted off toward the house.

"Listen," I told my friends. "Mom and Dad said we could actually sleep out in the tepee tonight, here in the yard, as long as we have Bobby with us." (Bobby is my beagle. Even though he has only three legs, my parents think he's Mr. Watchdog.)

"Way cool!" crowed Ariel, slapping high fives with me.

"Awesome," said Jasmine happily. "Okay, my name is Autumn Wind."

"My name is Nakoma," Ariel said.

"And my name is—" I began.

"Pocahontas!" my friends shouted.

You heard right, but you might not totally understand what they meant. It wasn't just that we were going to play Native Americans, and I would pretend to be Pocahontas. The explanation is both simpler and more complicated than that. And it all has to do with magic.

From the time I was really, really young, I could tell there was magic in my world. I saw signs of it everywhere: in flower buds bursting open in the springtime, in the way my dreams were so mysterious and yet told me so much. But I didn't understand the big picture until I saw the movie *Pocahontas*. That was what made everything snap into focus.

When I saw that movie, shivers went up my spine. Suddenly everything that I had thought or felt my entire life all made sense. In one amazing, almost scary moment, I realized I Pocahontas. Not just felt like. Not just seemed like. I mean, I really *am*. We are one and the same person. I can't completely explain it. But I accept it, and so do all my friends.

The thing is, all my friends are Disney Princesses themselves. Somehow, the same magic that made us aware of who we are inside also brought us together to be friends.

The first Disney Girl I met was Ariel. One day when I was six, I saw her trying to do a gutsy daredevil stunt on her bike. Right away we knew we were made to be best friends. She was already friends with Yukiko and Ella from her kindergarten class. (They were five years old when I was six. They're eight now.)

One day, while we were watching the video of *Pocahontas* at my house, I blurted out who I was. I took a chance on my friends. They didn't let me down. One by one they revealed their secret identities: Ariel was the Little Mermaid. Once she said it, I felt as if I had finally taken off my sunglasses. It was like, *of course!* She has bright red hair, blue eyes, a bunch of sisters, and swimming is her favorite thing in the whole world!

Before I had recovered from realizing that Ariel was Ariel, Yukiko announced that she was actually Snow White. The real Snow White. The princess. Her name even means "Snow Child" in Japanese! (She's Japanese-American.) And she has seven dwarfs of her very own: six younger brothers and a baby sister. Yukiko's best friend, Ella, admitted to being Cinderella. Back then, it was just her and her dad, but now she even has a stepmother and two stepsisters! (They all get along, though.)

So there we were: four Disney Princesses. Disney Girls. We had found each other, and knew we would be tight buds 4-ever. And as soon as we opened up to each other, even more magic came into our lives.

A year after that, Yukiko met Jasmine in her ballet class. Well, Yukiko could recognize magic when she saw it. After a couple of months of hanging out with Jasmine, we discovered that beneath Jasmine's blond hair, green eyes, and freckles, she's Princess Jasmine, from *Aladdin*!

And just last year, Isabelle transferred to Orlando Elementary from another school. We found out she lives here in Willow Hill, and she and Jasmine fell into total best-friend-dom. Who is Isabelle? Here's a test: Do you know anyone who reads all the time, loves French things, is really smart, and comes with her very own Beast? Uh-huh. Isabelle is Belle, from *Beauty and the Beast*. Her Beast is her next-door neighbor Kenny McIlhenny. (And he *is* really beastly.)

Now we're tighter than ever, and the secrets that magic wants us to know have been shown to us. Like, we all have special magic charms. (Mine is a silver feather.) We can make magic wishes. We can call on magic to help us do our best, or figure out what to do.

It's way cool. It's way Disney Girls.

Chapter Three

Fourth Grade Rules!

"That sleepover really rocked," Ariel told me on the school bus Monday morning. (All of us except Jasmine take the bus to school from Willow Hill. Jasmine lives in Wildwood Estates, and her mom usually drives her.)

"It was super-dee-duper!" chimed Isabelle in a high, corny voice.

We laughed. I had to admit, it had been pretty awesome. I was totally into it, of course, since we were in my world. We had set up my huge tepee, which my dad had designed and I had helped him build. We had all chosen

Native American—type names. We had even cooked our meal outside, on my parents' little grill! We'd made veggie kebabs (my family and I are vegetarians), roasted corn, and even s'mores. Then, with Bobby standing guard and keeping us company, we had flopped down in our sleeping bags and talked until we'd fallen asleep sometime after midnight. If only I could live that way all the time.

Now it was Monday morning. I know some kids don't like school, but Orlando Elementary is different. And my fourth-grade teacher, Mr. Murchison, is pretty hip.

Jasmine was waiting for us right inside the gates, as usual. Last summer we'd had a big scare when Mr. and Mrs. Prentiss had decided that Jasmine was old enough to head off to boarding school. We had all freaked out, then we had sprung into action. Jasmine had put together a multimedia demonstration to explain to her parents why she felt she wasn't ready to go to boarding school. When they had decided she was right, we partied for three days!

Now every time I saw her at OE, it seemed like a special event.

"Battle stations, battle stations," Ariel said when the morning bell rang. I laughed.

"See you at lunch," I told her. Ariel, Ella, and Yukiko

headed off to Ms. Timmons's third-grade class, and the rest of us pounded up the stairs to Mr. Murchison's room.

"Morning, everyone," he said after he took roll. "Today we're going to start a new unit about myths. Myths have been around almost as long as humankind has. They're a very basic, very important form of literature and of history."

I leaned forward onto my desk. This already sounded neat. That's what's so great about Mr. Murchison. He can always find what's interesting about a subject, and he doesn't treat us as if we're just kids. He challenges us, so we're never bored.

Mr. Murchison continued: "People have created myths to explain almost every aspect of human life. There are creation myths, myths to explain weather and earth conditions, myths to explain why people, plants, and animals are the ways they are. Many myths are tied to different world religions. Myths are one way people organize, explain, and explore the world around them. Now, can anyone name a myth they've read, or heard of?"

"'Brer Rabbit'?" suggested Lani Watkins.

"Nope," said Mr. Murchison. "'Brer Rabbit' is a folktale. I'll explain the difference in a minute. Anyone else?"

I thought about it.

Isabelle raised her hand. "How about things like the story of why there's day and night? The Greeks?"

"Yes." Mr. Murchison pointed his finger at her. "That's correct. But not all myths have to be ancient. There are modern myths—for example, Rudyard Kipling's story 'The Elephant's Child' is about why the elephant has such a long trunk."

"There are lots of Native American myths about nature and people," I said.

"That's right," said Mr. Murchison. "We've found that every group of people who live together for a long time— hundreds or thousands of years—create myths to help explain their experiences in the world."

I felt the familiar tingle of magic. That wasn't surprising. Magic is the thread that runs through everything in life. Ancient myths often had magical aspects. It made me wonder: was magic more obvious in olden times? Were "myths" really just factual tellings of real events? Maybe people nowadays were so caught up with busy, modern life that they had lost touch with the magic that's around everyone. That was what made being a Disney Girl so special. (Besides having five best friends.)

Mr. Murchison went on to read a few short myths to us. He read a Native American myth about why crows have black feathers and harsh cries. He read a myth about Anansi, the African spider. He read the Greek myth about Persephone, which explains why there's a winter and a summer each year.

When he had read several different myths, he gave us an assignment: each of us had to observe our world, then write a two-page myth explaining why something was the way it was.

"I don't get it," said Eric Morgenstein.

"You mean, like write a myth about why platform shoes are popular?" asked Allison Mason. (That girl is a walking fashion victim.)

"Ah, no . . ." said Mr. Murchison. "You'll notice that one thing all myths have in common is they explain things that are pretty much permanent conditions, like the appearance of animals, or aspects of the weather, or the shape of a mountain. Things that won't change very quickly, unlike a fashion trend."

"Oh," Allison said.

"So I want you each to closely observe your world, and choose one more or less permanent aspect of it," said Mr.

Murchison. "Then write two pages explaining why it's like that. If you need more help, come see me after class and we can discuss ideas."

Wow. My brain was already turning over with things I could write about. I love being outdoors, observing nature, being one with it. This assignment would give me a great excuse to really hang out outdoors and be in Pocahontas's world. I could hardly wait.

Chapter Four

Kee-Yah!

Okay, now, the thing about sparring in a tae kwan do class is that the object is not *necessarily* to beat your opponent. It isn't all about winning, which is one reason I finally decided it would be all right to do.

When I first started tae kwan do, it was by accident. Last spring all of us DGs spent a week at the Disney Institute, at Walt Disney World, here in Orlando. Each of us got to choose a weeklong class to take. I had signed up for rock climbing (one of my all-time faves), but our reservations got mixed up, and I ended up with Jasmine's tae kwan do class! (Jasmine had to take Isabelle's writing seminar, Ella took Ariel's acting class, Yukiko got my rock climbing class, Ariel suffered through Ella's cooking course, and Isabelle ended up liking Yukiko's gardening lessons! They all turned out to be the best mistakes we'd ever made, though.)

Anyway. I thought the idea behind tae kwan do was way cool, but the sparring thing bothered me. I am a very nonviolent person. I can't stand people arguing or fighting or being mean to each other. It really stresses me out. So the idea of whaling away at an opponent seemed like a major drawback. I talked to my two teachers, Sensei Kerry and Sensei Dasher, about it. They took the time to explain that sparring is an excellent way to learn different combinations and also your own limitations. Plus, it hones your skills at reading clues about your opponent. They convinced me that sparring can be a very useful learning tool.

In our dojo, we're taught to pull our hits, which means it's actually a fault if you hit your sparring partner with everything you've got. You're supposed to have enough control over what you're doing to be able to just *touch* your partner with your foot or fist. Each touch earns you a point. If you hit someone too hard, you lose points. Now I feel like some of my most important lessons have been learned during sparring.

So, on Tuesday afternoon Mrs. Prentiss gave Jasmine and me a ride to the dojo. Mrs. Prentiss hates the idea of Jasmine taking tae kwan do, which of course is one reason Jasmine enjoys it so much. But her mom is trying to be supportive, so she'll give us rides and help Jasmine buy all the equipment she needs.

It was a cool class on Tuesday. We started with basic calisthenics to get us warmed up, our blood pumping, our lungs working. We did push-ups and sit-ups and worked with weights to build strength. Then we practiced different punches, kicks, spins, and chops. We worked with the heavy bag: one by one, each of us would run forward and do a back spinning kick at the heavy bag, trying to hit the bag as hard as we could with the side of our foot. I love doing stuff like that. You have to put your whole being into that one kick.

I sprinted forward, judged where I should stop, switched my weight to one foot and spun backward, yelling "Kee-yah!" as loud as I could with a strong, forceful breath. Yelling at the moment of impact helps

21

you put all your effort into what you're doing. It also takes your mind off what it feels like when your naked foot hits a bag that weighs hundreds of pounds.

Sensei Kerry, standing behind the heavy bag and bracing it with her body, said, "Good, Ms. Paula."

I got back in line, pleased and breathing hard. (In the dojo, we all call each other by a title of respect, like Mr. or Ms., and our names. Using titles like that helps us to remember that we must always show each other respect. In class, Jasmine and I have to call each other Ms. Jasmine and Ms. Paula! We joke about it when we're outside of class. Another respect thing we have to do is to bow before we enter or leave the studio area of the dojo.)

Class was over at four-thirty. Jasmine and I changed in the girls' dressing room and put our gis and safety pads into our bags. We could hear the next class coming in. My shoulders automatically tightened when I heard Jam's voice.

"Baby belts all gone?" he asked, and someone with him laughed.

My mouth set in a hard line, I slung my duffel on my shoulder and stalked out of the dressing room. He was already in a crisp white gi, standing in front of the mirrored wall. He was knotting his blue belt around his waist with sure, deft movements. Suddenly he looked up and caught my eyes in the mirror. He gave me a cold smile, like the smile of a tiger.

I tried to keep my face completely smooth, and just kept walking on out the door. Inside, I have to admit, I was rattled. It isn't like I try to be Ms. Popular Girl, but I'm not used to people disliking me on sight. I had no idea what his deal was, but it was getting under my skin. I knew I would have to get to the bottom of this. But how, and when?

Chapter Five

Hello, Damon?

That night at home it was burrito night. You know, both of my parents work. My dad is an engineer. He designs bridges and stuff for the city of Orlando. My mom is a vet. She has an office with another vet. Both of their jobs are way hard and take a lot of time. On top of that, neither one of them has ever been into housework or cooking that much. While my mom was still in vet school, she was around more and did more stuff for us. Now that she works so hard, Damon and I pick up the slack.

Which brings me to burrito night. A while ago, my

family got tired of not knowing what to fix for dinner every night. We wound up eating sandwiches a lot, which is so lame. So during a family meeting we picked seven things that we all like to eat, and we fix one of those things every day. For example, today was Tuesday, so it was burrito night. On Wednesday, we have soup of some kind. Thursday means homemade or frozen pizza, Friday is stir-fried whatever, on Saturday we have some kind of rice-and-beans combo, on Sunday we experiment or have leftovers, and then on Monday we do a casserole.

It may sound like a big yawn to always know what we're going to eat every night, but actually it's worked out great. The different kinds of things are almost endless, so it's more varied than it sounds. The good thing is that Damon and I can take charge of getting meals together if we have to. It makes me feel really independent. Like I'm prepared for when I'm a grown-up.

I like burrito night because I can try cool new ingredients, like cilantro and salsa. One of my best burritos ever was black beans, yellow rice, chopped avocados, chopped cilantro, really spicy salsa, and shredded pepper jack cheese. Yum!

Pocahontas's Best Burritos

You'll need:

- 1 can refried beans, or some other kind of beans (I like black beans or pinto beans, too. I am not named after the bean, if that's what you were wondering.)
- 1 cup grated cheese (cheddar, American, or Monterey Jack are all good)
- 2 cups shredded lettuce (sometimes I use sprouts)
- 2 cups chopped vegetables, like tomatoes and avocados
- 1 package tortillas

First, warm up the beans and the tortillas. For each burrito, place one open tortilla on a plate, and spoon on some beans, cheese, and vegetables. Sprinkle on the lettuce. Add salsa sauce if you want.

Roll it up and enjoy. You can add practically anything else that you want, like rice, or peppers, or sour cream.

After dinner I logged on to our computer in the dining room and started to research myths. (We always eat in the kitchen, so my parents use the dining room for their offices. I like to do my homework there, too.) I got so many hits it took me a while to start sorting them. Mostly I wanted to read about the history of myths so I could decide what kind of thing I would explain in my own myth.

"Paulish?" said Damon, tapping me on the shoulder. I jumped.

"I didn't hear you," I said, putting my hand on my chest.

Damon grinned. "Us sneaky Native Americans," he said. "We're like cats."

To tell you the truth, I don't like jokes about Native Americans, even when Damish does it, who's a Native American himself. So I sat there stone-faced.

"Listen, Paulish," he said, "can you log off? I've been waiting to use the phone."

"I'm doing homework," I pointed out.

"I really need the phone," he said.

I looked at him. Basically, he looks exactly me, except bigger and a boy. But tonight he looked—different somehow. I couldn't put my finger on it.

"Ten minutes," I said, breaking the modem connection.

"Thanks." He looked relieved.

At that exact instant, the phone rang. Damon whirled and sprinted down the hall to the other phone. "I'll get it!" he yelled. Very unusual behavior for my brother.

So of course I picked it up on my end.

"Hello?" squeaked Damon, sounding strangled.

"Hello, Damon?" said a *girl*.

That was when I hung up. I grinned to myself. Did Damon have a *girlfriend*? Wait until the DGs heard about this!

Chapter Six

Practice Makes Perfect

"Stop it, Stopit," said Ariel, trying to push my cat off her chest.

It was Thursday, and Ariel had come over after school to help me practice tae kwan do. Or at least, I had *asked* her to come help me. What she was actually doing was lying on my bed reading some dumb fashion magazine.

"You know Stopit thinks any lap is fair game," I said, trying not to smile.

I cannot believe I've gotten this far without telling you about my pets. Okay, so I've mentioned Bobby, my beagle, and Meeko, my raccoon. But my family also has two other dogs: Jazzhot and Duchess, who are both rescued retired greyhound racers. And besides Stopit, who's a big, furry gray and white guy, we have Getdown and Nomore, who are also cats. My dad named them. Plus we have four little finches in a cage in the dining room, and my brother has fish in a tank in his room. Every once in a while we have a foster pet—an animal my mom is trying to fix up so it can be adopted. It's always hard because I fall in love with it and then get all bummed when we have to give it up. But so far my folks have said that eleven pets (not counting the fish) are more than enough.

"Please, Stopit," Ariel groaned, trying to push him off her chest again. But Stopit hunkered down and clung to her. Finally she gave up, and he settled in contentedly and started making muffins on her T-shirt. Ariel propped her magazine on his back and flipped the pages.

"You know, I need some more tank tops," Ariel said thoughtfully.

I was on my floor, stretching out my muscles before working out. Silently I rolled my eyes. I'm sorry, but I just can't get all worked up about clothes. I mean, who cares? If it fits and it's clean, it's good enough for me.

"And I have only one pair of platform sneakers—maybe I could use a red pair," she continued.

"Platform sneakers!" I snorted. "Please!" I stood up and then bent down, placing my hands flat on the floor and keeping my knees straight. "Like I'm so sure you could run, or jump, or climb trees in sneakers that look like they're on stilts."

"Hey!" Ariel protested, pushing aside Stopit's tail so she could see me. "They're adorable! And I need to get a few more things to complete my fall wardrobe."

I did some practice forward punches, blowing my breath out hard with each thrust. I paused for a minute and brushed my hair off my forehead. "Ariel, this is *Orlando*. There *is* no fall here."

Ariel made a face at me and went back to her magazine.

"Could you watch me do some katas, and tell me if you think anything looks awkward?" I asked her.

"Yeah." Ariel sat up, setting aside her magazine. Stopit grumpily rolled off her and started washing himself. "You sure are all into this karate thing," Ariel said.

"Come on, how many swim meets have I gone to?" I countered.

"You're right. Okay, start," she said.

I moved through my katas, starting with the very first one and working my way through the second, then the third, and the fourth one that I had to learn for my green belt. It took almost an hour, but Ariel sat patiently (a miracle for her!) and watched. Every once in a while she would ask me to repeat something, and once I messed up and had to start over because I had forgotten a step. It helped me, knowing she was paying attention. She didn't know what the moves should be, of course, but she's just as athletic as I am, and she could tell when something looked clumsy or off. She was a big help, and once again I thanked magic for bringing us together.

After I was satisfied that I knew my katas pretty well, I changed out of my gi, and we ran out into the backyard. In our yard we have three old willow trees, and one of them is my very own Grandmother Willow. It's a huge tree whose trailing branches actually reach the ground. The branches make a circular, hidden room where my friends and I can hang out in secret. It's where I go if I need to think heavily about stuff, or if I need to ask Grandmother Willow's advice.

Once Ariel and I had crawled beneath the branches and sat down, I spilled the whole story about Damon's weird phone call.

"A girl?" Ariel exclaimed, her blue eyes shining. "All right! Could this be a real girlfriend?"

"I don't know," I admitted. "It could be, or maybe it was just someone from his class asking for a homework assignment or something."

"Nah." Ariel dismissed that idea with a wave of her hand. "He was acting too weird for that. Unless he has a crush on her, but she doesn't even know about it and just thinks he's a friend."

We pondered the exciting possibilities for a while.

"This is so great," Ariel said. "Finally one of our siblings is starting to date—maybe. Let's see, Damon is fourteen, so he's the oldest, right?"

I shook my head. "Lucy's fourteen, too." Lucy Rogers is Ella's stepsister. "How old is Camille now?" Camille is Ariel's oldest sister. There's Camille, Laurel, Ariel, and Sophie. All of them but Sophie are on swim teams. Eerie, huh? Or *magical.*

"She's twelve," Ariel said. "Yukiko's the oldest in her family, Jasmine's an only child, and so is Isabelle. So it looks like it's up to Damon and Lucy to give us something to gossip about!"

I laughed. "It's strange to think about, but it's kind of neat too."

"I've decided I don't want to have a boyfriend until I'm like, twenty-five," said Ariel.

"Yeah? Why?" I asked.

"I've got too much to do," she said flipping her long red hair over her shoulder. "I've got this huge list of places I want to go, and I'll probably be a famous Olympic swimming champion by then, so I won't have time for guys. You know, with all my endorsements and commercials and spokesmodel stuff going on. And let's face it, most guys are totally lame."

I thought about Jam suddenly, and it was like the sun had gone behind a cloud. Why did he bother me so much? Why did he dislike me? Could Grandmother Willow help me to find the answers? I started to ask Ariel to help me make a magic wish, but just then my mom called me to come feed our pets. (We all take turns.)

"I better go, too," said Ariel, scrambling out from beneath the branches. "I'm going to be late for dinner, as usual. See ya tomorrow!"

"Later," I said. I had some thinking to do.

Chapter Seven

I Mythed It

"Find anything?" Isabelle whispered to me.

I sighed and shrugged my shoulders. We were at the Willow Hill library branch, researching myths. It wasn't my idea of how to spend a Saturday morning. I mean, I like to read, and I like doing well at school, but on Saturdays I LOVE to be outside, running around, skating, riding my bike—you get the picture. At least I had a tae kwan do class late this afternoon, so I knew I would get *some* exercise.

"I was looking for some kind of African myth that I

could adapt," continued Isabelle in a low voice. "But I haven't really found anything just right."

"Me neither," I said. "I was looking for a Southeastern Indian myth, but they all seem to be about fertility." I blushed. "I mean, no way!"

Isabelle giggled softly. We headed over to where Jasmine was poring over a book of Roman myths. She was twirling a strand of her long blond hair around her finger as she read. The three of us fourth graders were all trying to do our homework. The three third graders were just hanging out to keep us company. I could see Ella, Yukiko, and Ariel over in the reading section, and I wished I could join them. I was getting kind of worried about this myth assignment. I hoped I would have a brainstorm soon!

After two hours of stressing our brain cells, the six of us headed next door to Betty's. Betty's is one of the coolest places in Orlando, and it's right next door to the library, which is super convenient. Have you ever been in an old-fashioned soda shop, with little tiles on the floor, ceiling fans, mirrors, and a bar with stools? That's what Betty's is like. Lots of kids from school hang out there.

"Yes!" said Ella. "Our booth is empty!"

We always like to sit at the same booth, the one facing

the street in the front. That way we can see the action both inside and out. After we had ordered our usuals, I wanted to talk about Damon. (I usually get a fruit smoothie, Ariel gets a chocolate milk shake, Isabelle gets frozen yogurt, Ella gets an order of fries, Yukiko loves their onion rings, and Jasmine closes her eyes, stabs the menu with her finger, and gets whatever it falls on. Today it was a fruit salad.)

"So get this," I said. "I think aliens have kidnapped Damon. He's totally not acting like himself."

"Any more phone calls?" asked Yukiko. (I had told the DGs everything, of course.)

"He gets phone calls all the time, but I'm not sure if it's that girl or not," I reported.

"What's he doing?" Ella asked.

"For one thing, he's actually paying attention to how he looks," I said, giggling.

"That *is* something," Isabelle agreed. "I mean, if there's anyone who cares less about their appearance than you do, it's Damon."

I tossed a wadded-up napkin at her. "It isn't that I don't care about how I look," I said. "It's that I can't spend nine hours a day thinking about it!"

37

"Whatever," Isabelle said, grinning.

"Anyway, Damon's actually asked my opinion about what he's wearing, he spends hours in the bathroom, and I even heard him asking Mom if he could buy some new jeans."

"Whoa," said Jasmine. "That sounds pretty serious. I think he got through all of last year with two pairs of surfer shorts and three T-shirts."

I nodded. "He's branching out. I heard him mention close-toed shoes!"

"Too bad he has only you to ask for advice," said Ariel, immediately putting up her hands to fend off my attack. "Now, *I* could give him some *real* pointers."

"And the next thing you know he'd be trying to play basketball in platform sneakers and hair wraps, and all his friends would be laughing at him," I answered.

By now we were all laughing pretty hard. I was about to ask Isabelle if we should use her magic mirror charm to get a good view of what was going on with Damon, but Ella interrupted me.

"You know, I thought it was September, but it must

be spring fever happening six months too late," she said. "Because Lucy's doing all this same stuff."

"Lucy, the jock?" Isabelle asked.

"Yep." Ella nodded. "She actually left the house yesterday in a—get this—*skirt.*"

I gasped. I'm totally athletic, but Lucy Rogers is a jock with a capital J. She's on the All-Star soccer team at Orlando High, and she travels to meets all over the country. Plus she's training for the Orlando Young Triathlon, which was coming up in October. I had only ever seen her in workout clothes. The idea of her wearing a skirt was like so shocking.

"Oops, heads up," Jasmine said in a low voice. She made a small motion over her shoulder, and I followed where she was pointing.

It was Jam. Jam and some of his buds had just come into Betty's. I recognized a couple of them from the dojo, but there were a few I didn't know, also. All of a sudden my good mood evaporated. While I was looking at him, he happened to glance over at me. Guess what. He acted like he didn't even know me! I was about to give him a polite nod when he turned away, looking through me as if I wasn't even there. I felt my blood boil. Then I was bummed at myself for letting him get to me. Memo to Paula, I thought. Ask Grandmother Willow what his deal is, and soon!

"No, it isn't spring," I said dryly. "It's autumn, and I wish some animals would start hibernating!"

Chapter Eight

Grandmother Willow

"Paula!" I heard my mom call. "Paula!"

I shut my eyes tighter and tried to relax, which of course is practically impossible when you know you're supposed to be inside, helping your family clean house. Most Sundays, we try to make a dent in the mess that we can't deal with during the week. Mom had been cleaning the kitchen, Dad was doing laundry, I had been vacuuming, and Damon was dealing with the big, screened porch, which always tends to collect everything.

But all of a sudden, as I was sucking up some humongous

fur balls from under the family room sofa, I'd decided I couldn't wait for one more minute to talk to Grandmother Willow. All week, I had been wanting to get in touch with my magic, and I hadn't had a chance.

So I had escaped into the hot, sunny backyard and slipped beneath Grandmother Willow's comforting branches. Which is why my mom was calling me. "In a minute, Mom," I yelled. "I'll be right back."

I heard the back door close, and took a few deep breaths, trying to let tension out and let calmness in. It's true that magic is all around us all the time; but it's also true that if you don't slow down and pay attention to it, you might live your whole life without realizing that it is there. My life had been really full and active lately, and I felt that I had left magic behind. Not a good feeling.

But now I was taking time for *me*. The air was hot and stuffy beneath the tree, but at least I was in the shade. I could smell the grass, the warm earth, the tree. . . . I breathed in, I breathed out. I tried to clear out everything that was on my mind: Jam, my myth assignment, Damon . . .

It didn't take long before I felt a soft, cool breeze

swirling gently around me. I smelled spices and a refreshing scent of water. Gradually my muscles relaxed, like a wave smoothing sand on a shore. It was as if I had just woken up from a long, deep sleep full of wonderful dreams.

I opened my eyes. "Grandmother Willow," I breathed. Her branches swayed around me, as if she were gathering me in her arms. "There are so many things going on right now . . . I feel pulled in many directions." I was quiet, and then I heard her answer float into my mind: *Every path has trails that lead away. Some trails are good to follow. Choose trails that will help you learn.*

It wasn't like I heard an actual voice speaking out loud. I could just somehow sense it. Like most of her answers, this one didn't exactly turn on the defroster. I usually have to think and think about her teachings before I get what they mean.

I let more of my feelings out. "Grandmother, I'm troubled by my feelings about Jam. I don't like it when I don't like someone, and I hate it when someone doesn't like me. What's going on?"

I waited silently, listening to the sounds of nature. You might think there isn't much nature in a backyard, but there is. You just have to look for every little detail, and get into whatever you find.

We are afraid of ourselves.

When I heard Grandmother Willow's answer, I frowned. What the heck did *that* mean? I didn't have a clue to this one—it made about as much sense as "E.T., phone home."

"Paula!" called my mom. "I can't mop until you vacuum!"

I sighed, feeling magic evaporate. I was hot and sweaty and gritty from sitting in the dirt. "Coming!" I yelled back, and crawled out from beneath the tree. I felt . . . I actually felt *grumpy*. And I hardly ever feel grumpy. I mean, I'm not Little Ms. Sunshine all the time. I'm usually just *even*.

But I definitely felt grumpy right now. I decided to run with it. "Thanks a big, fat heap," I muttered to Grandmother Willow as I stomped toward the house.

I thought I heard her chuckling.

Chapter Nine

Jamming

On Monday the six DGs ate lunch fast, then ran far out into the school yard. We needed some privacy.

After we sat down, Ariel complained, "We're going to bake out here. Can't we sit under the pine trees, at least?"

I frowned at her. "Sure! Good idea. Then when we link pinkies and make a magic wish, all our friends can watch us and join in!"

Ariel lifted her long red hair and clamped it to her head with a butterfly clip. "I'm just saying it's hot, is all," she grumbled. "I mean, it's *September*, in *Orlando*. It's not like we live in *Maine* or something."

I immediately felt bad for being sarcastic. Ariel was right. It was boiling out here.

"I'm sorry," I said. I blew my hair out of my eyes. "I know it's hot. I'll try to make this fast." Quickly I told my friends what Grandmother Willow had said, and how I didn't get it. "Can we make a magic wish?" I asked. "Maybe if we're linked together, the answer will seem clearer."

Early on in our Disney Girl-dom, we found that if we're connected, our magic seems stronger. Whenever any one of us is troubled about something, we try to help by joining our magic with hers. Now it was my turn.

Trying to look casual, we linked pinkies and chanted:

"All the magic powers that be,
Hear us now, our special plea.
Paula's message seems unclear,
Please help the right path to appear."

We closed our eyes and sat silently, trying to let magic's answers flow to us.

Anger is not the path to follow.

My eyes popped open. Well, no duh! I felt like I was about to scream. (I usually *never* feel like that!)

"I know anger isn't the path to follow," I said in frustration. "I've always known that. But I can't help feeling angry at Jam—he's just so heinous!"

My best friends looked at me. Ariel reached out and patted my knee. "I know how you feel," she said. "People who act like that make me want to pound them."

"I don't want to pound anyone!" I cried.

"Maybe you do," Ella said. "And you just don't know it."

"Everyone wants to pound someone sometimes," Isabelle said.

I picked at my shoelaces. "Not me."

That afternoon, I took an extra tae kwan do class. After our regular class, Mrs. Prentiss picked Jasmine up, but I stayed for the next session.

The four-thirty class is for advanced belts. Lower belts are allowed to do what they can, and it was a good chance for me to get extra prepared for my green belt test.

As I did stretching and strength exercises with the rest

47

of the class, I was super aware of Jam doing the same things at the other end of the studio. I thought about what my friends had said, what magic had said, and what Grandmother Willow had said. But it was all still a jumble. The answer was floating in front of me like a feather, and I only had to reach out and grab it. But for some reason, I couldn't.

Some things in class I hadn't learned yet, so I sat and watched, trying to learn. I looked on as the kids did katas and paired exercises, wishing I could take part. When Sensei Kerry and Sensei Dasher demonstrated different things, I got a total rush. They're both awesomely good and strong, and I try to be as much like Sensei Kerry as I can.

Toward the end of class, our teachers set up sparring matches. The matches were supposed to focus on controlling your offensive moves. I sat back, ready to learn all I could by watching students more advanced then me.

To my surprise, Sensei Dasher motioned me forward. "Ms. Paula," he said in his raspy voice, "I'm pairing you with Mr. Jam. Mr. Jam, keep in mind that Ms. Paula is an orange belt."

"Yes, sir," answered Jam, looking at me with his cold

blue eyes. Adrenaline surged through me as we faced each other on the sparring mat.

(Before you get worried, let me tell you that we were both wearing foot guards, shin guards, arm guards, big padded gloves, and face and head guards. We looked like hockey players. It's all part of doing the sport safely.)

Jam and I bowed to each other. Then we began slowly circling the sparring mat, never taking our eyes off each other. For no reason, Grandmother Willow's voice floated into my mind. *We are afraid of ourselves.* Well, I thought, I'm not afraid of myself, and I'm not afraid of *Jam*, either. I moved in and threw a forward advance, which Jam dodged. I spun and tried a back kick. Jam blocked it easily. He punched forward, and automatically I threw up my arm and blocked it. I have to tell you, sparring is totally cool most of the time.

While I was thinking about how fun sparring is, Jam spun and landed a side kick to my stomach. He just barely touched me, but I was shocked—it happened before I saw it coming. Quickly I stepped back, knowing he had just scored points off me. He gave me a cold, superior smile, and I totally blew my cool. I got so angry, so fast, that without thinking I leaped forward in a strong roundhouse kick. If Jam had stayed in one place, I would have flattened him. (Which is NOT what sparring is about!) But of course Jam moved, which meant I flew through the air without control and landed heavily on my side.

"*Oof!*" The breath left my lungs in a painful *whoosh*. Even worse was the rush of mortified embarrassment that engulfed me. What had I done?

Jam was standing at attention at the end of the sparring mat. He knew the fight was over.

Everyone in the dojo was silent. I knew they were thinking about how foolish I had been. My cheeks flamed, and I got awkwardly to my feet, trying to suck air into my lungs and biting my lip to keep myself from crying.

Sensei Kerry strode over and briskly checked to see if I had hurt my ribs. "I'm fine," I croaked, gasping.

"Mr. Jam, four points," Sensei Dasher announced. "Ms. Paula, one point." He didn't need to say more. I was the loser—in more ways than one.

I hobbled over to the girls' dressing room. Inside, I sat down on a bench and wrapped my arms around my aching side. One hot tear escaped my eye and rolled down my cheek. Angrily I brushed it away as the door opened.

"You all right?" asked Sensei Kerry. "You took a pretty hard fall."

"I'm okay," I said, my voice breaking. I hated to have my teacher seeing me cry.

She sat down next to me on the bench. I started taking off all my guards—class was almost over and there was no way I was going back out for the last five minutes.

"Anger is your enemy," Sensei Kerry said quietly. "It will defeat you every time."

I was like, okay, get in line. Everyone in the whole world wants to talk to me about my anger. And I'm like the least angry person I know!

"Jam knows that," my teacher said. "When Jam was a white belt, he showed a great deal of promise—as you do. But he couldn't control his anger. He wanted to win all the time. An older student often goaded Jam into foolish actions. Until Jam learned to control his emotions, he couldn't get control of his body, and he couldn't advance into the higher ranks."

I stared at her. "Is that what you think I'm doing?"

"I think it's what you and Jam are doing together," said Sensei Kerry.

"So Jam hates me, just like that older kid hated Jam?" I asked.

Sensei Kerry got up to leave. "On the contrary. That older kid was one of Jam's best friends. And Jam is now a star pupil." Giving me a pat on the shoulder, my teacher left the dressing room. I sat there with a dazed look on my face.

Chapter Ten

Myth Pinto

All Tuesday night I wanted to lie on my bed in my room and think about me and my life and Jam. I wished Ella would make me a list of everything I had to figure out. (Ella makes lists for everything! We tease her about it sometimes.)

But I had something else staring me in the face. (Besides Meeko, I mean.) My myth for Mr. Murchison.

I had done lots of research, but nothing had grabbed me. Here it was, the day before the paper was due, and I had zilch. Zero. Nada. I groaned out loud, and Meeko looked up. He was sitting on my desk, where he had opened my pencil drawer. He was taking out all my pens and pencils and throwing them on the floor. That's the kind of thing he does.

I scooped him up and cradled him on my stomach. He sat on his haunches and played with my hair, combing it with his front paws. He's so cute! For about the thousandth time, I wished I were an animal. Animals don't have homework assignments, or classes with difficult people in them.

Meeko slid off me, waddled over to the door, and pulled it open. I heard his little claws clicking as he went down the hallway. In a few minutes he came back, holding a soggy graham cracker. Which meant he had somehow opened the package of them in the kitchen, washed one in the sink, and was now going to eat it in my room, making a big mess. I couldn't even get worked up about it. I had bigger problems.

My magic silver feather charm was on a slim chain around my neck, and I held it in my hand, hoping for . . . a magical brainstorm? A miracle?

Then it came to me. The answer floated into my mind as I sat there holding my charm. Bits and pieces came together, and then all at once I saw the path I had to follow. And my myth began to write itself. (Not literally. But you know what I mean.)

How the Sparrow Proved Its Strength
By Paula Pinto

Once, when the world was young, all the animals everywhere ate fruit from the same tree. Through spring, summer, fall, and winter, the tree bore fruit, the fruit fell to the ground, and the animals ate the fruit.

One summer, for some reason the fruit did not fall to the ground. The fruit stayed on the branches, until the branches hung so heavy the animals feared they would break.

The animals got together to figure out how to solve this terrible problem.

"I will shake the tree!" said the gorilla. He seized the tree in his huge hands and shook with all his strength. But the fruit stayed on the tree.

A small sparrow, watching, wanted to

55

provide food for her friends. She was very small and light, and did not know what she could do. But she decided to try anyway. "I will shake the tree!" she said in her tiny sparrow voice. So she grabbed the thick trunk in her little wings and shook it. Of course the tree didn't budge.

A rhino plodded forward. "I will knock down the tree!" This would kill the tree, but the animals were desperate. The rhino charged and butted the tree with all his strength. The tree didn't budge.

"I will knock down the tree!" cried the little sparrow. She ran at the tree and butted it with her head. She hit the tree so hard that she knocked herself out, but the tree didn't feel it.

"I will climb the tree!" said a squirrel. She raced to the tree and started to climb, but soon slid down again. The tree's bark was so smooth and shiny that the squirrel couldn't hold on.

"I will climb the tree," the sparrow said

groggily, and lurched toward it. She did not get even one inch up the trunk. Her wings were not designed to grip things.

The animals were getting more and more hungry. "What will we do? What will we do?" they moaned. "There is not one of us who is strong enough to get to the fruit."

The sparrow was very bummed to hear this. She had wanted to prove her strength, but had only made herself look foolish. She looked down at her small brown wings and frowned. These dumb wings! They could not shake things, they could not climb, they were only good for . . . flying.

"I will get the fruit!" the sparrow cried.

The other animals laughed. "How can you? You are so small."

"I will," promised the sparrow. Then, taking a deep breath, she flapped her wings and took off. Easily and gracefully she flew into the air, then circled the tree. She was so small she could fly right between the thick branches. Her feet could grasp a twig perfectly. She sat on a twig, and with her little beak pecked at the stem of a piece of fruit. Soon the heavy fruit dropped to the ground.

The animals were amazed. "More! More!" they shouted.

The sparrow stayed up in the tree, pecking off one piece of fruit at a time, until the sun went down. Below her, the animals ate their fill.

At last the sparrow flew down to her friends. They had saved a juicy piece of fruit for her, and she began to eat it.

"You were right, Sparrow," said the rhino. "You did it, and you saved us all."

"Even though you are not very strong," said the gorilla, speaking with his mouth full.

"I have strong wings, and a strong brain," said the sparrow. "And best of all, I am a sparrow." And she went back to eating her fruit, which had never tasted so delicious.

The end.

There. I was finished. It didn't explain rainbows or volcanoes or anything like that, but I hoped Mr. Murchison would like it. I liked it a lot myself.

Chapter Eleven

Friend Against Friend

Guess what. I got an A-minus on my myth. I was happy with my grade, but there were a lot of other myths that I thought were so awesome. Like Isabelle's myth about the differences between boys and girls—whoa! All the girls thought it was great. All the boys were making dumb jokes about girls (typical). I loved it.

Once the whole myth assignment was over, I could really concentrate on tae kwan do. Today was Thursday—the belt test was Saturday. My friends were going to come to the test, and so were my parents. I had asked Damon, but frankly, he had hardly been around lately. The girlfriend mystery was continuing, but I was still without a clue. I knew she had to be way cool, though, if Damon liked her.

After school on Thursday, I rode my bike to the dojo. (It's only about half a mile from Orlando Elementary.) Jasmine was at ballet. I wished she were with me.

Inside, I saw a crowd of kids standing in front of the bulletin board. They were looking at the belt test schedule! I waited till I could get closer, then eagerly pushed my way to the front. Six people in my class were taking belt tests: Jasmine, a boy named Harry, another boy named Malik, and I were taking tests for green belts. Two other kids were going for their orange belts. At some point, we'd have to work our way through rounds of sparring. These lists showed who would be sparring whom.

Quickly I scanned the lists. I cross-checked them. I frowned. I found my name and Jasmine's, but surely something was wrong. I did the calculations in my head, and worked my way through the rest of the lists.

It was as if a huge black storm cloud had settled on my

shoulders. I don't know how I got through the rest of class, but when it was over, I called an emergency meeting of the Disney Girls.

"I guess you're wondering why I called you all here," I said, making a lame attempt at a joke. It was Friday afternoon after school—the soonest we could all meet.

"I am, for sure," said Yukiko. "But first, does anyone want a snack?"

Everyone did. I waited as Yukiko took drink orders and fixed a tray with cheese and crackers and yummy Japanese seaweed snacks. (Don't knock them till you try them. They're really good.)

In the meantime, Yukiko's six little brothers were getting in our way, grabbing their own snacks, fighting with each other, zooming toy planes around in our faces, yelling, spilling things, standing with the fridge door open, losing things, getting upset, knocking into Yukiko, etc. Yukiko didn't even seem to notice. I guess she's gotten really good at tuning them out. Her little brothers aren't monsters or anything, but there are six of them, so it gets a little intense. I'm so glad (we all are) that Snow White's seventh Dwarf was a baby girl.

"Hi, Mom," said Yukiko, balancing the tray on her hip and leading the way down to her room.

"Hi, guys," said Mrs. Hayashi. She held baby Suzie on her shoulder. Baby Suzie turned around, smiled at me, and gave a little baby burp. She was so cute! I smiled back at her. My problems seemed a weensy bit lighter after seeing her smile.

In Yukiko's room, we sat on the floor and dug into our munchies. Her room is the total opposite of my room. My room is full of pictures of horses, pictures of people doing tae kwan do, and sports equipment and stuff from nature.

Yukiko's room looks like Laura Ashley's idea of heaven. It's really, really girly and froufrou, with violets on the wallpaper, lavender flowers on her sheets and comforter, lace, ruffles, more lace, more ruffles—if I had to live there, I would get kind of twitchy. But it suits her fine.

"Okay now, what's up?" Ella asked.

"It's about tae kwan do," I said. "I read the sparring lists, and get this: if Jasmine and I win our first rounds in our belt tests, we'll have to spar against each other!"

I got five blank stares. Isabelle took another cracker and crunched her way through it.

63

"And?" Ariel prompted me.

"And nothing!" I said. "I don't want to spar against Jasmine!"

Jasmine took a sip of lemonade. "What do you mean?"

I stared at her. "You're one of my best friends! I don't want us to spar each other!"

To my amazement, Jasmine laughed. "Why not?" she said. "It would be fun!"

I must have had an *X-Files* look on my face, because Jasmine continued in an imitation of Sensei Kerry, "Ms. Paula, sparring is a learning tool. We learn from each other all the time. It's not like we would be trying to hurt each other."

"But one of us has to win!" I said.

Jasmine cocked her head and looked at me. "Really?"

I couldn't believe it. I had fallen into the trap of wanting to win the match. But sparring isn't about winning, or defeating your opponent. It's about doing the best you can in that situation.

I put my hand over my mouth. "Oops," I muttered.

"Uh-oh," Jasmine said, grinning at me. She put her hands together and bowed low to me, as if we were in class. "You have taken the wrong path, Grasshopper," she said in a singsong tone. "You must let go of your desire to win. You must do the best you can, but without anger, or pride."

Boom. It was as if a jolt of lightning had flashed into my brain, showing me everything I needed to know. I had been all caught up with the idea of winning, mostly so I could beat Jam someday. And why? Maybe because he reminded me of myself. *We are afraid of ourselves.* I was angry at him for being so good and so arrogant at the same time. But maybe I had been that way too—trying to be the best, to be better than anyone. Even better than one of my best friends.

"I have to be a sparrow," I said wonderingly. If I could just be my regular Pocahontas self, maybe I could let go of my competitiveness. And the way cool thing about how magic works was that as soon as I got the message, as soon as I understood what was happening, I felt my anger and tension melt away, as if blown away by a breeze. I was myself again, for the first time in two weeks!

"Hey, yeah," said Isabelle. "You have to be a sparrow."

"What the heck are you talking about?" Ella asked.

I explained about my myth, and about the magical message I had just understood.

"See," I told the DGs, "I was so focused on getting my

green belt that I spaced on the real goal: to improve my skills. It isn't about defeating others—it's about doing my best."

Jasmine nodded. "Very good, Grasshopper."

I made a face at her, and we laughed.

"Thanks, you guys," I said. "I feel like I'm on track now. Now I don't even mind that if I score highest in all my sparring matches, I have to spar against Jam."

"What?" Jasmine shrieked.

I laughed.

Chapter Twelve

Go, Jasmine, Go!

Saturday morning. The day of our belt test. I felt calm, cool, and collected. On the outside I might have been wearing a crisp white gi and my orange belt, but on the inside I stood tall and proud in my Pocahontas dress with my silver feather charm. A true princess of power. I tried to let magic flow through me. I kept focused on my goal.

I wasn't even aware of my parents, Damon, and the rest of the Disney Girls as I took my place in line. All of us, the whole school, from white belts to black belts, moved through our katas, in choreographed movements. It felt as if I were in a beautiful, graceful ballet.

The white belts stopped after the first kata. The yellow belts stopped after the second kata. Jasmine and I and the other orange belts did the third kata, and then those of us taking the green belt test continued through the fourth kata.

With each motion I tried to stay focused in the moment, feel the magic, and remember that I was a princess. It felt fabulous.

After the fourth kata, we stood aside as the higher belts kept going through their forms. I watched Jam and refused to feel angry. He did very well with his katas, as usual. Once he met my eyes and his gaze narrowed. I looked back at him evenly. I looked forward to what I could learn from him.

Then it was time for the sparring matches.

Four matches took place at the same time. First it was Jasmine against a girl named Elizabeth, me against Malik, and two other pairs. Jasmine scored higher than Elizabeth, and I scored higher than Malik. Next Jasmine sparred with Harry and I sparred with Frannie.

We each scored highest. For the next match, we would have to face each other.

When Sensei Dasher clapped his hands, we each stepped to the edge of the sparring mat. I looked deeply into Jasmine's eyes, and she looked into mine. I saw Princess Jasmine, with long dark hair, dark eyes, and olive skin. It was fun to think about sparring against one of my favorite princesses, and I smiled. She smiled back. Then Sensei Kerry gave the command. The sparring match began.

Although Jasmine and I had practiced sparring together a little bit, it was nothing like this. We lunged, we withdrew, we circled. I punched and she blocked; she kicked and I blocked. The weird thing was, even though we were sparring against each other, our moves were so in tune that it felt like we were working together to create something special. It felt great.

Finally, when we were both breathing hard and had strands of hair sticking to our damp foreheads, I anticipated one of Jasmine's moves. As fast as I could I shot my right foot out and touched Jasmine lightly on the ribs. Her eyes lit up, impressed. I grinned at her. And the match was over.

"Ms. Paula, five points," said Sensei Dasher. "Ms. Jasmine, four points. Excellent match, ladies."

Panting happily, Jasmine and I rushed together and gave each other a big, big hug.

Chapter Thirteen

Destiny Knocks

I knew it would happen, and it did. Jam and I ended up facing each other on the sparring mat. He tried giving me his cold stare—I gave him a cheerful smile. He muttered something about baby belts, and I blew on my fingernails and rubbed them against my gi, unconcerned. That was when he started looking worried.

"Begin," said Sensei Kerry.

With Jasmine the two of us had moved as if we were in a ballet. If I was doing ballet with Jam, it must have been some fierce battle scene from a ballet about warriors. Jam

71

seemed determined to win this match, whether that was the point of sparring or not. He was taller than me, and weighed more, and was much more experienced. In my heart, I expected him to score higher. But I kept focused, paid attention to my breathing, and let my magic flow. I just wanted to do my best. I didn't feel one drop of anger.

Even though this match was a bit tougher and rougher than the one with Jasmine, still, I had a fabuloso time. I felt like a machine on autopilot, blocking punches, blocking kicks, lashing out with my own punches, chops, and kicks when I could. He managed to land a touch twice, and I (to my amazement) landed two touches also. We blocked, we parried, we circled, we sweated. My eyes were locked on his, brown onto blue, and I just let myself spar as best I could.

I was startled when Sensei Dasher clapped twice, signaling the end of the match. Surprised, Jam fell back, his arms at his side. He looked as bewildered as I did. Then I realized Jam must have won.

"I'm calling this match a draw," said Sensei Dasher. My eyes opened wide. "You both sparred extremely well. You have the same number of touches and the same number of errors. Your scores are equal."

My mouth opened—I couldn't help it. I had been gearing up for this for a month, and here it was. I had done well.

"Ms. Paula, Ms. Jasmine, Mr. Malik may all come forward to collect your green belts," said Sensei Kerry. "Mr. Harry may retake the test next month."

My green belt! I was a green belt! Proudly Jasmine and I knotted our new belts around our waists, then gave each other high fives. We waved and smiled at our families and the DGs. Damon looked very proud of me. It was a great moment. And someday, I knew, I would be collecting my black belt. Someday.

"Excuse me, Ms. Paula," said a voice.

I turned to see Jam holding out his hand. "Congratulations," he said. "You fought great."

I shook his hand. "You mean great for a baby belt?"

He smiled at me. "I mean great for any belt. You're a worthy opponent."

Well. Those words meant a lot to me, I have to tell you.

"Hey, you want to go for pizza?" Jam asked.

"Uh, uh," I stammered.

"With the rest of the dojo?" he continued.

"Can my friends come?"

"Sure." He smiled. He motioned toward the door. "After you, Paula Pinto."

"Oh, no, after you, Jam . . ." I began, but I realized I didn't know his last name.

"Smith," he supplied. "John Michael Smith. J.M. Jam. Get it?"

John Smith.

I almost fell over.

Chapter Fourteen

A Mystery Revealed

My folks and Jasmine's folks said it was okay for us to get pizza with the rest of the dojo. They gave us rides there, and said to call them when we needed to be picked up. I felt really stylin'.

"So are your parents proud?" I asked Jasmine as we walked into Little Ricky's Pizza Haven.

"Yeah," Jasmine said. "I mean, I bet they still wish I was doing only ballet, but at least they admit that tae kwan do isn't as bad as they thought it would be."

75

Inside, we saw that Sensei Kerry and Sensei Dasher had pushed together about ten tables to form a long line. Our dojo had practically taken over the place! Isabelle, Jasmine, and I sat on one side in the middle of the long line, and Ella, Yukiko, and Ariel sat across from us. Kids from the dojo swarmed all over, grabbing chairs. Guess who sat next to me?

Jam.

"That was so awesome, Paula," said Ariel, unwrapping her straw. "You looked so warrior-girl."

"Thanks," I said, pleased. I looked at the menu, trying not to feel self-conscious that Jam was sitting right there.

"What are you going to get?" he asked.

"She always gets the vegetarian special," Yukiko informed him.

"Hey, me too," said Jam.

"You're a vegetarian?" I almost squeaked.

"Yeah," he said. "My whole family is."

"Mine too," I said. This was getting scarier and scarier.

"Bonus," said Ariel, smirking at me. I knew what she was thinking: Paula and Jam, sitting in a tree, K-I . . .

I narrowed my eyes at her, sending her mental "Forget it!" signals.

"Extra pepperoni and mushroom," Isabelle decided, and Jasmine agreed.

Last week, Jam was my biggest headache. This week, he was maybe becoming one of my friends. I found out he was in sixth grade at Orlando Middle School, and he liked the Casey Brothers, and he had an older brother named Andrew who was in seventh grade.

All through this, five pairs of fascinated Disney Girl eyes were boring into us, watching us as if they were watching a tennis match. I made a mental note to talk to them about it later.

"Hey, it's Damon," said Isabelle, nodding toward the door.

I looked up. "That's my brother," I told Jam. Then I watched in amazement as a girl came through the door and took Damon's hand. A girl! Holding my brother's hand! In public!

"That must be her!" I blurted, before my brain had finished processing the info it was receiving.

"That's Lucy!" Ella gasped.

The six of us looked at each other, our mouths hanging open like fish. Damon, my brother, and Lucy Rogers, Ella's stepsister, were in Little Ricky's Pizza Haven holding hands. They were boyfriend and girlfriend.

"Whoa," said Ariel.

"I can't believe it," Ella breathed. "Lucy almost looks normal."

"Lucy and Damon," I repeated, still in shock. I looked at Ella, and she looked at me. "My brother, and your stepsister."

I grinned.

Ella grinned back. "It's practically magical," she said.

"Yeah," said Ariel. "But is it good magic, or bad magic?"

"I guess we'll find out!" I laughed.

Here's a sneak preview of
Disney Girls
#11 *The Gum Race*

"Ella O'Connor, please see me after class," said Ms. Timmons.

For a moment I was so shocked I didn't even respond. Then I mumbled, "Yes, ma'am." I sat back in my chair, my face burning. I could feel my friends' eyes on me—Ariel and Yukiko, looking at me in solemn support. I couldn't believe it. Me, Ella O'Connor, in total trouble with my teacher! This kind of thing had never happened to me before.

For the rest of the period, I sat hunched in my seat feeling mortified. I could hardly pay attention to what was happening in class, but Ms. Timmons didn't call on me—not once. I was so humiliated.

And I knew just who I had to blame: Rob Taglieri. My eyes narrowed, and I felt anger replace the fire of embarrassment. It was all Rob's fault. And meek, mild-mannered little Cinderella was going to make him pay. . . .

Read all the books in the
Disney Girls series!

#1 One of Us

Jasmine is thrilled to be a Disney Girl. It means she has four best friends—Ariel, Yukiko, Paula, and Ella. But she still doesn't have a *best* best friend. Then she meets Isabelle Beaumont, the new girl. Maybe Isabelle could be Jasmine's best best friend—but could she be a *Disney Girl*?

#2 Attack of the Beast

Isabelle's next-door neighbor Kenny has been a total Beast for as long as she can remember. But now he's gone too far: he secretly videotaped the Disney Girls singing and dancing and acting silly at Isabelle's slumber party. Isabelle vows to get the tape back, but how will she ever get past the Beast?

#3 And Sleepy Makes Seven

Mrs. Hayashi is expecting a baby soon, and Yukiko is praying that this time it'll be a girl. She's already got six younger brothers and stepbrothers, and this is her last chance for a sister. All of the Disney Girls are hoping that with a little magic, Yukiko's fondest wish will come true.

#4 A Fish Out of Water

Ariel in ballet class? That's like putting a fish in the middle of the desert! Even though Ariel's the star of her swim team, she decides that she wants to spend more time with the other Disney Girls. So she joins Jasmine and Yukiko's ballet class.

But has Ariel made a mistake, or will she trade in her flippers for toe shoes forever?

#5 *Cinderella's Castle*

The Disney Girls are *so* excited about the school's holiday party. Ella decides that the perfect thing for her to make is an elaborate gingerbread castle. But creating such a complicated confection isn't easy, even for someone as super-organized as Ella. And her stepfamily just doesn't seem to understand how important this is to her. Ella could really use a fairy godmother right now. . . .

#6 *One Pet Too Many*

Paula's always loved animals, any animal. Who else would have a pet raccoon, not to mention three cats, three dogs, four finches, and fish? When Paula finds a lost armadillo, though, her parents say, "No more pets!"—and that's that. But how much trouble could an armadillo be? Plenty, as Paula discovers—especially when she's trying to keep it a secret from her parents.

#7 *Adventure in Walt Disney World:* *A Disney Girls Super Special*

The Disney Girls are so excited. The three pairs of *best* best friends are going to spend a week together at Walt Disney World. Find out how the Disney Girls' magical wishes come true as they have the adventure of their lives.

#8 *Beauty's Revenge*

Isabelle is thrilled when she finds out that her beastly neighbor, Kenny, will be going away on vacation for a week with his family. Then Kenny comes down with chicken pox—and he has to stay at Isabelle's house for the week! She might be tempted to feel bad for Kenny—if he wasn't being his usual beastly self. With the help of the Disney Girls and a little magic, she decides to give Kenny a taste of *her* own medicine.

#9 *Good-bye, Jasmine?*

Jasmine has always been a little bit different from the other Disney Girls. She lives in the wealthy Wildwood Estates instead of in Willow Hill like her friends. But at least the girls get to see each other every day at Orlando Elementary. Then one day, Jasmine's mother decides that it's time for her daughter to attend her alma mater, St. John's boarding school. The Disney Girls are in shock. Will they have to say good-bye to one of their best friends?

#10 *Princess of Power*

Ever since her first class at the Disney Institute, Paula has loved the challenge and fun of tae kwan do. She and Jasmine are steadily working their way up the ranks to be green belts. But there is one cloud in an otherwise sunny horizon: Jam. He is another student who seems to have taken an instant dislike to Paula. His behavior brings out feelings of anger in Paula that she doesn't like at all. Can magic help show her how to work things out?

#11 *The Gum Race*

Ella loves having Ms. Timmons as a teacher. She is so cool that she lets them chew gum in her class every Friday! That is, until Rob Taglieri decides to play a trick on Ella that gets the privilege revoked. Now the whole class is mad—at Ella! So she decides to run for class president to bring back Gum Fridays. But if she doesn't, her new political career could be over before it begins. . . .

#12 *The Divine Miss Ariel*

Everyone knows that Ariel has a great voice—after all, she's Ariel! Now the school is having a holiday celebration, and every class is going to perform. There are a few singing solos, and Ariel just knows she is going to be chosen for one. When auditions are over, though, she is shocked to find out that not only does she not have a solo, but she has been demoted to a totally unglamorous role! But Ariel wouldn't be Ariel if she didn't have a backup plan. . . .